THE FAST AND THE FEAST

Forty Lenten Meditations

THE FAST AND THE FEAST

Forty Lenten Meditations

K.M. George

2019

The Fast and the Feast: Forty Lenten Meditations– published by the Rev. Dr. Ashish Amos of the Indian Society for Promoting Christian Knowledge (ISPCK), Post Box 1585, Kashmere Gate, Delhi-110006.

ISBN: 978-93-88945-07-3

Laser typeset by

ISPCK, Post Box 1585, 1654, Madarsa Road, Kashmere Gate, Delhi-110006 • *Tel:* 23866323

e-mail: ashish@ispck.org.in • ella@ispck.org.in
website: www.ispck.org.in

Contents

Contents

Introduction

Observing forty days of prayer and fasting (Great Lent) in preparation for commemorating the sufferings and crucifixion of Jesus Christ (Passion Week) and finally celebrating his resurrection (Easter) is an ancient practice of the Christian Church. The believers are expected to pass spiritually through the various experiences of Christ himself so that they are renewed in body, mind and spirit. Repentance and renewal leading to "a new creation in Christ" (2 Corinthians 5:17) is the major focus of these observances.

Pressures of modern life have eclipsed to a great extent the significance of the practice of Lent. But there are signs of a renewed interest to return to the wisdom of an age old tradition. Medical, psychological, environmental and social sciences now attest to the values of moderation in consumption, self-discipline, simple life-style, mutual forgiveness and care for the common good. Balancing the

Fast and the Feast and re-attuning to nature's rhythm are essential for the survival of all life on the planet earth.

Just before he started his public ministry Jesus went alone to the desert. In total solitude and dedication he observed an intense 40-day tapas of fasting and prayer.

Jesus went through all terrible human temptations, but did not yield to them. He overcame the material desires of body and mind, anxiety and greed, lust for power, fame and possessions. He emerged as the compassionate one - healing the sick, lifting the downtrodden, consoling the afflicted, protecting the weak, caring for poor women and children, and announcing the Good News of the reign of God. Finally he gave himself up on the cross for the salvation of the world.

The simple meditations in this book were composed day by day during a Lenten period. They are not primarily academic biblical-theological expositions. Instead they are experientially drawn from the traditional Lenten practice of meditating on the Word of God through the prayers and rituals of the ancient Syriac liturgical tradition as practised in the Orthodox Church in India. The rhythm, music and colours of nature form the inevitable backdrop for these biblical-liturgical meditations. The author deeply shares the ancient insight that it is in God's creation that we first listen to the creative Word of God and partly experience mysteries hidden to the wise and prudent of this world but revealed to little babies (Luke 10:21).

My deep gratitude goes to the colleagues at ISPCK particularly to the General Secretary and Director, Rev. Dr. Ashish Amos; Mrs. Ella Sonawane and Mr. Sundeep Chawdhry, for their support and encouragement in publishing this little book promptly at the time when we are about to begin another Lenten pilgrimage.

Fr. K.M. George
Kottayam
February 2019

Day One

The Feast

The mango tree in my neighbour's garden is already blooming. There is a delicate fragrance in the air. A host of honey bees and other flying insects swarm the tree. It looks like spring in temperate climates. But it is the onset of hot summer here in Kerala, south India. The air is getting warmer every day and is unbearably humid too.

We begin the holy Lent and set out on a journey that lasts for forty days and then the Holy Week - altogether fifty days until Easter. Let us begin with joy and hope. We set our hope on Resurrection as the destination of the journey and we have in us the joy of the Risen Christ by anticipation.

True, the Lent focuses on repentance. But we repent not in despair and bitterness but in hope and the joy of forgiveness. We have read and meditated on the passage from St. John's gospel where Jesus turns water into wine at the wedding feast in Cana. A wedding feast, of course, is an occasion of celebration and rejoicing.

The "sign" that Jesus did there was a sign of the Kingdom of God that unravels a new order of life. It was a pointer to the transformation of our human nature. Yes, we can change, we can be different human beings positively. Our communities also can change. So let us drink the vintage wine of joy that Jesus prepares for us amidst all the anxiety and the deep sense of guilt and shame and the unexpected shortage of resources at home.

We now focus on the joyous feast and the tree in blossom. But we need to wait patiently for the fruits. They appear slowly, ripen gradually, and after several months we will have delicious mangoes in enchanting colours and tastes.

Let us start the Lenten journey together. It is a pilgrimage. There is great value when we make the pilgrimage together, in the community, for the community and with the community in love, joy and peace.

Day Two

The Forgiveness

With the day's summer heat on, I notice from my window that several different birds, big and small, come to my little pond. They drink water and take a quick bath. No bird is afraid of the other though they belong to different species. I wish I could join them to splash water and do a little swimming. But if I go there they will all fly away. Why this mistrust and fear between me and the rest of creatures?

With this question in mind I went to the Devalokam chapel to join the Lenten Prayer of the Hours and the Service of Forgiveness (*Shubkono*).

In the gospel reading we heard the parable of the unmerciful servant who received the great kindness of his master, but was very unkind to his own debtor and fellow servant (Matthew 18:23-35). After the gospel reading, the leading priest knelt and prostrated before the people assembled for prayer and asked for forgiveness for his sins and shortcomings. The worshipping community in turn prostrated and asked the priest for blessings and the grace to forgive.

It is interesting that in the ordinary non-sanskritised Malayalam language the verb *porukkuka* used in the prayers has three meanings: to forgive as in 'Forgive us our debts as we forgive our debtors', to heal as in healing a wound or diseases, and to dwell as in dwelling together in one house. Forgiveness is the key to healing and the basis for human social life, human culture and human survival.

So *Shubkono* calls for love and peace beginning with mutual forgiveness. This is essential for the continuation of the world and survival of the human race.

It is the hardest thing, I admit, to be able to forgive. 'Forgiving from the heart' (Matt. 18:35), is certainly difficult for most of us. Still, let us take the first step in all humility asking God for the power of the Holy Spirit that we may walk in the path of *karuna* that ancient Indian word denoting compassion, kindness, mercifulness, tenderness and forgiveness as the essence of religion.

The Fast and the Feast

Day Three

The Communion

"After he had sent them away, he went up on the mountain by himself to pray. When evening came, he was there alone".   Matthew 14:23

(Matthew 26:36; Mark 1:35; 6:46; Luke 5:16; 6:12; 9:18; 9:28; John 6:15)

Every year, sensational books are in the market in the west that claim to resolve the mystery of the "hidden years" of Jesus. Some would say that Jesus was in Kashmir and that he learned advanced yoga techniques from Indian gurus during those years. That is why, according to them he walked on water and performed many miracles. But in the four Gospels, there is no trace of evidence about Jesus travelling abroad and acquiring esoteric knowledge. They portray him as a Galilean Jew who hardly knew any language apart from his native Hebrew and Aramaic the lingua franca of west Asia at that time.

The modern sensational writers and media are almost silent about the nights he spent alone in solitude in the hills and valleys of Palestine. It was a routine for Jesus that during the day time he would walk around with the disciples and teach the people, but in the evening, he would leave everybody and go away to solitary places in the lap of nature. What was he doing there throughout the night? Even his close disciples had no clue. So, they simply reported that in the evening, Jesus departed to a lonely place and spent time in prayer in communion with his heavenly father. We have no idea about the content of his prayers, whether he slept at all during those nights under the starry heaven with wild olives and figs as his only witness. We can simply guess he was in communion with the source of all that existed and with the virgin nature around. He must have prayed with loud words and deep sighs, with incessant tears and in profound silence. He must have been sitting or prostrating poses or simply lying down on the meadow or over rocky surfaces.

The two-fold communion of Jesus to God the Father and with nature was essential in realising his mission as the Messiah. It is quite likely that during the hidden years between the burgeoning teenage and the youthful maturity at thirty, he had already cultivated this practice of solitary nocturnal meditations. What the Gospel writers reported was, likely, the continuation of his longtime practice of meditation. This experience of communion with God and nature was the source spring of Jesus' ministry of compassionate identification with the poor, the sick, the downtrodden and the alien.

It is strange that in later Christianity, no real emphasis was put on the contemplative Jesus. Nor did it develop techniques of meditation like in India for instance. In the third century when the monastic movement started in the Egyptian and Palestinian deserts, we see some remarkable examples of solitary, contemplative monks. But the mainstream Christianity, particularly in its Roman imperial version, spent most of its energy and concern on visible and tangible matters that conformed often to the agenda of the world.

In the 1960s, when many young people in western Europe and America set out on a spiritual search to India and some other Asian countries, traditional Christians could hardly digest it. That was the time when the western world became exceedingly self-confident about the emerging scientific -technological "paradise" and it mercilessly exploited natural resources without any scruples to the fatal detriment of the environment. Secularisation arising from economic and technological self- complaisance dethroned God and underestimated spiritual values. Much of official Christianity that remained became too anthropocentric and hostile to nature. It ignored subtle and deeper spiritual aspirations of the inner person. It was in this context that sensitive young people made a massive exodus to the east.

Lent is a time when we need to reflect seriously on what we humans have done to break the vital relationship between humanity on the one hand and with nature and God on the other. Actually, this hidden web of inter-connections was by us in the past. We may take the analogy of the hiddenness of the spirituality of Jesus not only during the eighteen years but throughout his life until his very end on the cross. Even on the eve of his death on a tree, he went to the olive garden of Gethsemane in the night to be in communion with his heavenly Father for the final accomplishment of his messianic mission.

Day Four

The Face

This afternoon I went to see the well-known artist-sculptor Kanai Kunjuraman and view his emerging new work the Mother-Letter in front of the Kottayam Public Library. He has been working hard in the scorching sun with his team of workers for a year now to finish the gigantic sculpture. We usually meet once a week. Lately, he appeared to be brooding and meditative. Obviously he was worried about the final outcome as he was giving special care to touch the face of the Mother-Letter. This afternoon when I shared with him my sincere opinion that the Mother's face was coming out more and more alive with dignity and grace, his face brightened up with a discreet smile. One doesn't need to be an art critic to tell the beauty of a face.

A major orientation of the Lenten fasting is to seek the face of God. True, it is a metaphor, but a beautiful and meaningful metaphor. There is much in the image of the face. Adam and Eve were hiding from the face of God once they sinned. Yet God sought after them, and invited them to come out.

Now is the time to unveil our faces in a flood of tears before the face of God. Remember the heart-rending prayer of the Psalmist:

"Do not hide your face from me."   Psalm 27:9

Almost all human beings are born under the loving gaze of a maternal face. Even children born blind would sense what a mother's face is. Let us not imagine the face of a severe taskmaster or an unkind judge who watches us with the intention of finding fault with us or punishing us. Unfortunately, much of our religion consists in the fear of being judged and penalised.

The face of God Jesus revealed to us is just the opposite. Look at the face of the father figure in Jesus' parable of the Prodigal Son. He had been looking out to the gate for years with deep yearning and compassion to see if his deviant son ever returns. Look at the anxiety-ridden face of the shepherd who is desperately searching for his lost sheep, just one among a hundred. Look at the mother hen who hurriedly gathers the chicks under her protective wings when the predator eagle appears in the far corner of the sky above.

Let us believe in Jesus who shows us the tender face of God, in the promises of life and salvation that he has given us. Let us walk this pilgrimage gazing at the face in tears and hope.

Day Five

The Appetite

In the early 1980s, I was invited to be a resource person at a youth camp in Kuala Lumpur, Malaysia. The participants were Orthodox Christian young people of the Indian Diaspora from Malaysia and Singapore. In the week-long camp they served very good food. However, after two days some boys complained about the food and there was some discussion among the campers. The next morning as we entered the meeting hall, we found a sentence written on the black board: "When you are really hungry any food is good food." Later we found out that it was written by one of the participants, a girl in her early teens.

The difficulty with food is that even if you are fed the best food in the world continuously for several days, you are likely to develop satiety and begin to complain. The taste of food is a very relative one. In states of deprivation or satiety, the taste buds respond differently to food.

For many Christians food is a major issue during the Lenten period. Why should one abstain from this and that? How do we survive without essential nourishment from meat, fish and eggs? Will the brain of school-going children be weakened? Will they develop some deficiency or diseases?

Food was a major issue for Jesus too. He abstained from all food and drink for forty days, a remarkable feat for a human being. But when he successfully finished the arduous journey, Jesus began to be subtly assailed by the Tempter. He knew he was hungry, and everything there in the desert appeared to be potential food. He only needed to say a word and all the infinite number of stones would become delicious food. Jesus was hungry enough, but he refrained from performing that feat. He relativized the vital value of food in reference to the life-giving Word of God.

"One does not live by bread alone, but by every word that comes from the mouth of God." Matthew 4:3-4

Material food alone does not sustain us in our quest to become true human beings. Human economics and welfare schemes, however, make us believe the contrary.

Lent is a period not simply for our personal spiritual improvement, but also for the Church to review and re-order the very socio-economic and cultural "form of this world" in which we are unknowingly trapped.

"Do not conform to the pattern of this world"

Romans 12:2

We can break it by the power of God, and we should. "Another world is possible" as they say in the World Social Forum.

Day Six

The Lilies

We sat on mats spread out under the Peepal trees on the bank of the river Phalguni in South Karnataka. We were some 25 priests together with Bishop Yacob Mar Elias of Brahmavar diocese. I was supposed to assist in some sessions of the Lenten retreat of the priests out in plain nature. The beautiful river front was very quiet and deserted except for three sand-mining workers and some storks and other birds on the other side of the river.

We started with a small field exercise. Everyone was asked to scout around and find a wild flower each, small or big, in ten minutes. At the beginning we thought there would be some five to ten different flowers at the most in that small patch of grassy, sandy bank of the river. When we came together we counted up to 31 different flowers. Most of them were extremely tiny. We began our meditation on what Jesus said on the lilies of the field:

> "And why worry about your clothing? Consider the lilies of the field, how they grow: they neither toil nor spin. Yet I tell you even Solomon in all his glory was not dressed as beautifully as one of these."   Matthew 6:28-29

Yes, we had collected the lilies of the field, more than thirty Solomons with their glorious regalia! They are too small to be noticed. People usually ignore them. We trample them under our feet . Most of us do not even see these as we walk over them. Yet, take one of these and place it under a microscope or take a picture with a special magnifying lens. You will be amazed at the intricate design and magnificent colours embedded in those tiny, unimpressive wild flowers.

Think of the comparison which Jesus makes between the wild lily and King Solomon. It would appear ridiculous to our modern sophisticated minds. How can a negligibly small flower of the field be more splendidly arrayed than the great Solomon in all his royal glory?

Yet, this is how Jesus looked at everything in this world. It is the regard of the heavenly Father, the Creator God who stoops down to lift the poor and the needy and to care for every humble thing (Psalm 113:6). Jesus shows us that " the small is beautiful".

Let us try to follow this model to shape our Lenten regard, our perspective on God's creation. Can we also stoop down and see the small people - poor, miserable, afflicted, oppressed, helpless and dying in despair. They are out on the margins of the society, the unimpressive and the unwanted, trodden underfoot by those with wealth and power.

Day Seven

The Paradise

We climbed down the steps leading to the large pond in front of the ancient temple of Sringeri . The Mutth, the monastery of Sri Sankara, the great Advaita philosopher who founded the four seats (Peeth) of Vedic learning in the 8th century AD, is close by. The pond, open to the river, is teeming with hundreds of big Holy Fish. They are playful and not at all scared of the curious visitors who feed them with popcorn and bread. The fish come close to us; we can touch them; children play with them. We saw a woman gently stroke the head of a huge fish as if she is caressing her own child. The fish, like a dolphin, seemed to enjoy the touch of affection and tenderness.

Imagine all the animals, birds and reptiles that we now describe as wild and dangerous mingling with us in playful joy and intimacy. Adam and Eve had this experience in the Garden of Eden before they sinned. Adam was asked by God to give names to each one of the creatures in the world. We know that naming a child is an act of love and hope. We dream of a great future, bright and joyful, when we name a child. So Adam had a cosmic experience in which not only human beings but all creatures lived together as one family.

Referring to the scenario of the world after the flood the Book of Genesis reflects the Word of God:

"The fear and dread of you will fall on all the beasts of the Earth , and on all the birds in the sky, on every creature that moves along the ground, and all the fish in the sea."

Genesis 9:2

What a terrible situation! The relationship of friendliness and harmony between human beings and the rest of creation suddenly turns to fear and dread, and consequently to violence and bloodshed.

Lent is a period when we meditate on the paradise bliss of life that we lost because of human sinfulness. So we repent. But our repentance is not simply for our personal sins and shortcomings only, but for the restoration of the whole order of creation back to its pristine joy and perfect communion with God and with all of God's creation.

We sing in the liturgy of the Hours during the period of fasting:

> "The doors of Paradise are opened by the Lent. Those who observe it well shall receive the brightness of angels and the wings to soar up to the heights."

Day Eight

The Wake-up Call

A friend of mine called me this afternoon after a long interval and queried about my health etc. I complained to him that there was too much work - writing assignments, meetings and travel, and I had no time to rest and look after 'my own things', nobody to assist me, and I had aches and pains all over, the usual stuff that we tell people close to us ! My wise friend told me that I should be thankful to God for being fully occupied because what we usually imagine as rest and quiet is a pretext for laziness. Being a busy lawyer, he knew what he was talking about.

Lent is a wake-up call. It repeatedly exhorts us to shed laziness and be wakeful. The day has come when you should work hard in all righteousness, we sing in the night prayer of Lenten Monday:

'O lazy one, get up and shake off your slothfulness and earnestly work in the garden. Jesus calls you to the work of repentance, and even if you work only for the last hour you will still get the same Dinar, the full reward of life.'

Work in this context is repentance (metanoia) and all its fruits in our everyday life in terms of acts of love and compassion as well as our spiritual disposition to everything in the world. One is never late to get to work. Every moment is the appointed time (*kairos*).[1] So now is the time.

The work here is obviously different from the work that we do in our everyday life.

Jesus was fond of telling us the parable of the faithful servant in its different versions.

Alertness is the quality of the true steward. He does not know when the master will return, whether in the middle of the night or in the early morning. So the faithful steward is ever ready to receive him, and present him his accounts while the unfaithful one takes this unpredictability as an occasion for a wayward life and the squandering of resources.

Lent has the recurring theme of the End: the end of the world, the end of one's individual life. This is the uncertain dimension that urges us to be constantly watchful.

> "Therefore, you also must be ready; for the Son of man is coming at an hour you do not expect".   Matthew 24:44

In the Indian Hindu-Buddhist tradition our awareness can reach enlightenment once for all, like in the case of the Buddha. In the Christian tradition, a complete turning around, metanoia or conversion, can happen in our awareness as in the life of St Paul. However, in the case of ordinary mortals, we need to continuously cultivate this awareness and vigilance. It is work. It is also grace, the power of the Holy Spirit who graciously enables us to remain ever wakeful to God's gift of forgiveness and joy.

---

[1] *Kairos* is an ancient Greek word. The ancient Greeks had two words for time *chronos* and *kairos*. *Chronos* refers to chronological or sequential time whereas *kairos* means the right or opportune moment.

Day Nine

The Touch

I n the evolutionary scale the sense of touch is more ancient than
seeing and hearing and other sensory systems. It is also more
universal. While our other senses are located in one specific
part of the body, namely the head, the sense of touch is spread out
all over the body. Even those who are born blind and deaf perceive
the world through the sense of touch. Natalie Angier describes
touch as "the first sense aroused during a baby's gestation and the
last sense to fade at life's culmination."[1]

> "A leper came to Jesus begging him, and kneeling he said
> to him, 'If you will, you can make me clean'. Moved with
> compassion, Jesus reached out and touched him. "I am
> willing, He said, "Be clean." Immediately the leprosy left him
> and he was made clean."   (Mark 1:40-42).

Forbidden by the Law of Moses, touching a leper was a shocking
violation of the Law in the time of Jesus. But Jesus did precisely
that. Those of us who are familiar with the story of untouchability
in India in the past (and still lingering in certain pockets) would
understand the revolutionary character of Jesus' gesture.

---

[1] The New York Times, December 8, 2008.

Touching is an act of extending your body. In principle, whatever you touch becomes part of your body. When a mother touches and caresses her baby, she is passing the message: you are my body. She would feel it in its primal, literal sense since the baby was in fact part of her physical body for nine months or so.But this maternal touch can be expressed in many ways by people in different contexts. When a compassionate and competent physician touches the body of the patient, it can become a healing touch. The patient becomes part of the body of the healer physician. When a husband touches the body of his wife with love, or vice versa, 'they will become one body' as the Scripture says. Jesus could have healed the leper with a word at some distance. But he deliberately approached him and touched him and made him a part of his own body. This gesture brought deep healing since the social exclusion of the leper was even more painful than the disease itself.

Touch can be for grabbing and possessing, for exploiting and humiliating, for suppressing and eliminating life. Unfortunately, this is the kind of touch we are more used to. From domestic violence to genocide the evil touch haunts us everywhere.

Lent is a time when we particularly make an effort to sanctify our sense of touch, to make it a touch of love and compassion. Remember that human beings are the only species who can abuse the sense of touch. Let us take our bodies and minds to Jesus Christ our heavenly physician who will touch us with deep compassion and the power of healing.

Day Ten

The Prostration

Prostration is a common sight in India. Disciples prostrate before their Gurus. Devotees prostrate before the images of their favourite gods and goddesses. In its complete form prostration is *sashtanga namaskara*, veneration with eight limbs of the body touching the ground. The prostration or *kumbidil* during prayers in the Indian Orthodox tradition also makes use of the eight limbs (forehead, nose, two hands, two knees, two feet) in an act of repentance, humility and total submission to God's will and loving care.

The Orthodox worshipers are traditionally taught to bring to mind the crucified figure of Jesus as they prostrate in prayer. Though the general practice of prostration is declining, it is still strictly practised in monasteries and seminaries. However, during the period of Lent and the Holy Week many devout people practice prostration in prayer.

The book of Revelation describes an arresting scene of prostration.

> "The twenty-four elders fell prostrate before the One seated on the throne, worshiped the One who lives through out all the ages, cast their golden wreaths before the throne and chanted to Him: worthy are you, O Lord, worthy are You,

The Fast and the Feast

O God to receive glory and honour and power. You alone created all things, and through Your will and by Your design, they exist and were created." Revelation 4:10-11

This is probably the core of Christian practice of prostration, raising glory and honour to Almighty God and joining the hosts of angels who sing Holy, Holy, Holy to God.

There are many pious interpretations which are all acceptable as far as they help build up the Church, the Body of Christ, and our personal spiritual life. There is a strong component of humility and self-abnegation in prostrating before God. In the spirit of worship, we prostrate only before God, the Triune mystery that is incarnate in Jesus Christ. We will not bow down before any other power and principalities of this world. In the sense of worship, we will not prostrate before any human being however exalted in power and glory, and however spiritual in appearance. God alone is worthy of our worship.

But there is also the sense of veneration and honour in prostration. We bow our heads before venerable people as a matter of courtesy; we touch the feet of our Gurus as a matter of custom and deep respect. It does not mean that we raise them to the status of God.

Our Lord Jesus Christ teaches us to be humble. "For everyone who exalts himself will be humbled, and he who humbles himself will be exalted" (Luke 14:11). St Paul follows it up and tells us:

"Do nothing from rivalry or conceit, but in humility count others more significant than yourselves. Let each of you look not only to his own interest but also to the interest of others." Philippians 2:3

Lent is a time to practise humility like Jesus, the Word of God who "made himself nothing, taking the form of a servant."

Touching the ground with the forehead and other limbs is also a reminder that 'we are dust and unto dust we shall return'. But in our Christian understanding this is not the final end. We shall rise from the dust and shall participate in the glory of the risen Christ. The Lenten pilgrimage leads us on to that glory.

Day Eleven

The Display

It may seem paradoxical that the Lenten prayers exalt and denounce fasting in the same breath. Day by day the prayers portray to us the examples of Moses and Elijah, who fasted for forty days and received great rewards. Above all we have the supreme model of Jesus who fasted for forty days and conquered the temptations of body and mind.

Prayers declare that abstinence from food is trivial and of no spiritual value unless accompanied by acts of love, forgiveness and compassion. For many people observing the Lenten fast is simply abstaining from certain types of food like meat, milk products and eggs.

One of the essential readings is the passage from the book of Isaiah (58:1ff) where the prophet is severely critical of the fasting practised by many in his time. The prophetic Word of God accuses the fasters that they exploited their workers on the day of fasting; their fasting often ended in quarrels, strife and physical violence to each other. The prophet attacks also those who display publicly the external signs of fasting such as bowing their heads like a reed, and spreading out sackcloth and ashes around them. Then God's word says:

> "Is not this the kind of fasting I have chosen to lose the chains of injustice and untie the cords of the yoke, to set the oppressed free and break every yoke."   Isaiah 58:6

Jesus obviously takes this up in his criticism of the Pharisees and Scribes:

> "When you fast do not look sombre as the hypocrites do, for they disfigure their faces to show others they are fasting."
>
> (Matthew 6:16. See also Luke 4:16-1).

Lenten prayers try to bring home to us the true spirit of fasting. That is why they paradoxically advocate and denounce fasting at the same time. We need to maintain this self-criticism as essential for our spiritual growth. It is a real danger for us that we unknowingly tend to display to others our fasting signs while we forget about the real purpose and outcome of fasting.

The Fast and the Feast

Day Twelve

The Radiance

It is a delightful sight to see the morning rays of the sun fall on tender leaves on tree tops. The semi-transparent leaves appear radiant. But the more mature leaves are apparently less capable of letting the light through. The older they get, the harder to be penetrated by light!

Lenten prayers refer again and again to the luminous face of Moses. As narrated in the book of Exodus, Moses went up on the Mount Sinai to the presence of God. He received the Ten Commandments from God for the people of Israel though the Scripture says that on Mount Sinai Moses entered into thick darkness. He probably did not see anything in our usual sense of sight.

When he came out of darkness to the people below they found that the face of Moses was brightened up. When Moses came down from Mount Sinai with the two tablets of the covenant law in his hands, he was not aware that his face was radiant because he had spoken with the Lord. When Aaron and all the Israelites saw Moses, his face was radiant, and they were afraid to come near him. (Exodus 34:29-30)

It was not ordinary light that illuminated the countenance of Moses, but the reflection of the glory of God on the face of the one who went through a period of intense fasting focused on the desire to see God.

Lent is a Journey of forty days like that of Moses, when our whole being is focused on receiving the light from God. It is not simply the end point of the journey that is important but also the way and the walk.

Suppose you lost your way at night in a deserted place. Then you see a small flickering light at a great distance. You begin to take steps forward in great hope. The more you approach the light the more enlightened your face becomes. In desperate darkness immediately around you, you never take off your eyes from the distant light.

For Moses the enlightenment was happening gradually. He was on the way to the presence of God. In our case too climbing the mountain slope in the Lent period is a gradual process of approaching the unapproachable Light. It is hard and painful but it will certainly brighten up our face and heart. We have testimonies for saintly persons like Catholicos Baselios Geevarghese II of the Malankara Orthodox Church and Seraphim of Sarov of the Russian Orthodox Church whose faces became radiant even for fleeting moments, according to contemporary witnesses.

But most of such experiences happening to saintly persons are hidden to public knowledge. Even Christ's own transfiguration was not open to all the twelve apostles, but only to three chosen ones, even that under strict order of secrecy.

The Fast and the Feast

Day Thirteen

The Elements

One of the Lenten *sedra*-prayers says that Jesus fasted for forty days in order to strengthen the four elements of the universe which have become loose and weak due to human sin. It continues to state that human beings who are also constituted by the same four elements are strengthened ten times by the 40-day fasting of the Lord. Every element in the human person is made whole so that the human being becomes holy.

In ancient Greek cosmology, adopted by most Christian Fathers, the four elements are earth, water, air and fire. In Indian cosmology there are five elements. We have space (akasha) in addition to the above four. The patristic interpreters seem to play with the number four in different ways.

In modern cosmology one of the major questions is: what holds the universe together? With the countless billions of stars, planets and galaxies moving apart in an inflationary mode according to some theorists, the mystery of the smooth functioning of the whole is astounding.

Orthodox Christian theology would teach that it is the love and will of God that hold all things together in harmony. The weakening of the fundamental forces that hold the universe together is a spiritual problem. To say that Christ died for our sins has cosmic implications when we affirm that the fasting of Jesus was meant to reinforce and restore the fundamental elements of the universe. This applies in a very particular way to the human person who in his/her body contains all the elements that constitute the universe.

Lent emphasizes that in order to strengthen our body, mind and spirit we need to rediscover their spiritual origin. We are created in God's image, out of God's love and will. Our face represents the face of God's creation; our consciousness represents the God-consciousness spread out in all creation in an extremely subtle way. Since we are the image of God we need to represent God's face to the rest of creation as well.

Let us therefore hold out the hope on behalf of all creation, and dedicate our body, mind and soul to their original source, namely, God's love and will. St Paul tells us:

> "We know that the whole creation has been groaning in labour pains until now: and not only the creation, but we ourselves, who have the first fruits of the Spirit, groan inwardly while we wait for adoption, the redemption of our bodies."
>
> Romans 8: 22-23

The Fast and the Feast

Day Fourteen

The Paralysis

O n Sunday after the Holy Liturgy I visited an elderly lady - once a highly placed professional woman, now completely paralysed and bedridden. Holy Communion was to be administered to her. Upon my asking whether she was conscious, her family members told me that she was not really aware of much. But while praying at her bedside and giving her Communion in liquid form I found her really conscious though she was totally unable to speak or move her limbs. I saw her eyes swell with tears about to flow down her cheeks. The intensity of her inner feelings was obvious. Without any word or gesture we were able to communicate with each other.

In the liturgy of Holy Qurbana that morning (third Sunday of the Lent) we had just read and meditated on the gospel narrative of Jesus healing the paralytic (Mark 2:3-12). My encounter with this woman drove home an underlying message from the gospel account: the paralytic brought to the presence of Jesus by four people was sharply conscious of his condition, his surroundings and above all, his past.

Jesus, 'having seen the faith of those brought him', addressed not those helpers, but the paralytic directly:

"Son, your sins are forgiven."   Mark 2:5

Apparently, the man was waiting to hear these words. He must have reviewed his life, recognized his shortcomings and made some internal reparations for his sins during the period of his illness. This is why the word of forgiveness from Jesus brought immediate healing to him.

No scientific medical text would connect sin to disease. The great success of modern medical science in diagnosis and treatment is due to the discovery of the cause of most of our illnesses, particularly the physical ones. The moral or theological concept of sin has nothing to do with it.

In this biblical incident of the paralytic, forgiveness of sins is the clue to healing. Jesus in other instances would absolutely deny any connection between an individual's misfortune or illness and his/her sin. In certain psycho-somatic conditions, however, a divine healer like Jesus could discern such hidden connections.

However we should not quote the above example nor apply it in a general sense to judge anyone or make any unfounded assumptions in the case of individuals. What we can recognize at the most is the connection between humanity's collective sinfulness right from Adam and the human predisposition to disease in general. Let us not forget that sinless, innocent babies also are infected by disease. They too suffer and die.

Sin is paralysis in various degrees. Lent is the time to humbly recognize our own personal sinfulness and our great need for healing in the compassionate presence of our Lord Jesus Christ, our "heavenly Physician".

The Fast and the Feast

Day Fifteen

The Weapon

Disarmament is a familiar word for us. In the present context of the powerful weapon industry, with its scandalous international arms deals and the accumulation of lethal weapons by nations as well as terrorist organizations, many good-willed leaders and movements call for disarmament. With flourishing production and trade in weapons of mass destruction (WMD) the world of ordinary human beings is scared to the core. Even poor nations spend incredible amounts to buy weapons while their people starve, and malnourished children die in thousands.

So, it is a little bit disconcerting when the prayers speak of Lent as a powerful weapon. Yes, we are asked to turn to a re-armament. It is a recurring theme in the liturgical prayers. In fact, this is borrowed from the biblical language. In the New Testament, the weapon is spiritualized. St. Paul tells us :

> "Put on the full armour of God so that you can take your stand against the devil's schemes. For our struggle is not against flesh and blood, but against the rulers, against the authorities, against the powers of this dark world and against the spiritual forces of evil in the heavenly realms."
>
> Ephesians 6:11-12

We are asked to wear the spiritual weapon against all forces of evil. As human beings with free will and a great number of options to choose from, we are constantly bombarded with temptations of all kinds. So we need to take a courageous stand with the help of constant inner prayer, fasting, observing of silence, renouncing of certain addictive habits and so on.

In our Orthodox tradition, we are taught to make the sign of the cross on our body as a spiritual weapon, to fight the subtle promptings of the evil one. The Cross of Christ brings us to the presence of the Crucified Christ, who with his death and resurrection overcame evil and death. So every time when we pray, we make the sign of the cross on our body beginning with the forehead, continuing to the chest and then the left shoulder, and ending with the right shoulder. As the cross is the sign of protection for us we are empowered in our fight against evil.

Let us teach our little children this beautiful sign of salvation early in their life. Let young fathers/mother make the sign of the cross on the forehead of their babies in the morning as they wake up and in the evening when they are put to sleep so that they will be deeply marked by the great sign of victory over the powers of evil.

> "Stand firm then, with the belt of truth buckled around your waist, with the breastplate of righteousness in place, and with your feet fitted with the readiness that comes from gospel of peace. In addition to all this, take up the shield of faith, with which you can extinguish all the flaming arrows of the evil one. Take the helmet of salvation and the sword of the spirit, which is the Word of God." Ephesians 6:14-16

Most peace and disarmament movements are unable to achieve much probably because they are unable to provide any alternative to human lust for arms, violence, power and profit. Putting on the full armor of God - truth, justice, peace, faith- is the only alternative means for ensuring peace and *ahimsa*[1] in our world.

---
[1] Non-violence

The Fast and the Feast

Day Sixteen

The Field

Rice is the staple food for the people of Kerala. But ask the younger generation of Malayalees[1] whether they have ever observed at close quarters the process of cultivating rice - the arduous and meticulous process of preparing the ground and the seeds, the act of sowing the seeds and watering the field, the weeding and the waiting, the happy harvest and the gathering of paddy. Most young people will answer in the negative. In our generation we have nearly stopped cultivating rice in many parts of Kerala, and started importing our daily food.

When Jesus told the people in Palestine the parable of the sower, (A sower went out to sow his seed ... Luke 8:5-8) everybody understood the imagery immediately.

The Lenten prayers adopt the image of the field from the agricultural parables of Christ. The forty days stand for the field of history. It is also the field of our life span. We are the farmers. How are we going to use the field?

If we entrust an arable piece of land to a good farmer, he knows what to do with that. With his sweat and labour he would convert it to a fertile field where he can sow the seeds.

---

[1] People of Kerala who speak the Malayalam language.

There are several different uses of the metaphor of the field in Jesus' teachings. One of them is to consider the field as representing the needy world - the world of hunger and poverty, the world of conflict and quarrel, the world of injustice and oppression of the poor. What do we do with that kind of field when we are in a period of fasting and prayer?

We usually expect a beggar to come to the gate of our house and stretch his hands to us so that we can give charity. This gives us a sort of self-satisfaction. We imagine that we have done our duty and that we are going to get the heavenly reward. A Lenten hymn denounces this attitude. It says:

> "Do you expect the field to come to the farmer to be cultivated? Is it not rather the farmer who goes out to the field, carrying the seeds, in order to cultivate it? Therefore, you must not wait for the needy persons to come to you, but on the contrary, go out to them, and look after those who are in need and distress."

This reminds us of the shepherd who goes out at great risk to look for the lost sheep. This is the basis for Orthodox Christian ethics and pastoral care. We run the risk of becoming self-complacent about our fasting and prayer, the austerities we practise etc. We would then assume that we are the righteous ones, and all the world should come to us. In fact, the Lenten prayers exhort us to take the other attitude: The world is the field. Our life span is the field. We should earnestly go out with the seeds of justice and truth, care and concern for the people in need. We should make use of every day of our life span to practise compassion and bring joy and peace to the world in need.

> "For God so loved the world that he gave his only begotten Son ."   John 3:16

The Fast and the Feast

Day Seventeen

The Heart

"He who was sent from the Father's heart to the (heart of) creation, who dwelt in the womb of the blessed Mother full of grace..."   from a Sedra prayer of Great Lent

W e are familiar with the phrase "the heart of the matter". It is the crux, the essential point of something. In most cultures the heart is given great prominence as the centre of deep human emotions. We continue to use attributes like hearty and heartfelt to indicate the depth of one's sympathy and sincerity, and 'heartless' for the contrary. Yet we know that the heart is not physically at the centre of the human body nor does it have anything to do with our emotions, feelings and other psychological states.

The mystery of the incarnation of Jesus Christ is a heart to heart matter. The Son is eternally begotten from the heart of the Father, and historically begotten from the heart of creation, from the womb of a Virgin, the womb of created reality. The heart and the womb signify the mystery of life. When there is no heart, there is no emotion, no compassion, no empathy and therefore no human life can survive. When there is no womb it is the end of human life.

Our consumerist culture, in fact, denies both the heart and the womb though it pretends to promote both. All its propaganda and machinations, all its flamboyance and seductive charm alienate us from genuine human qualities of the heart and the womb.

Lent is a time to perceive the "the heart of the matter", to distinguish between the essential and the non-essential. How much food we need to lead a decent life with consideration to others who are deprived of sufficient food? How many different kinds of food we need to lead a healthy and happy life? To what extent are we sharing our food with those in need? These are some of the simple questions we need to ask.

Our global consumerist culture would never encourage us to ask these questions. Instead it would give us the message that we need more and more, that we need many different types of food, and expensive exotic food too to have a happy and respectable life. In my little town of Kottayam in the far corner of India we can buy kiwi fruits imported from Australia and grapes from California. Of course, only rich people can afford to buy them. Still the question is: do we need them for a decent life in a place where an enormous variety of local fruits are available. We have mangoes, bananas of all kinds, papaya, guava, jackfruit, passion fruit, chikku, pineapple and the list goes on.

Food stands as a symbol for all our ways and styles of life. The Lenten question is: what is the heart of our living as Christians, as human beings, as neighbours, as citizens? How do we sustain the womb of creation from miscarriage?

Our present day ecological crisis as well as our genetically modified products slowly lead us to sterile wombs, both human and non-human.

During Lent we are called upon to train ourselves from overuse and selfish exploitation of nature's resources by reducing our excesses in consideration to those in need, and to the future generations. The resources of our planet earth are desperately limited. The question again is: how much do we need to have a reasonably good life?

Jesus Christ our Lord says:

> "Therefore, I tell you, do not worry about your life, what you will eat or drink; or about your body, what you will wear. Is not life more than food, and the body more than clothes?"
>
> Matthew 6:25

Day Eighteen

The Twilight

"The night is almost gone, and the day is near. Therefore let us lay aside the deeds of darkness and put on the armour of light."   Romans 13:12

Twilight is the state of semi-darkness between night and day, either at the break of dawn or after sunset. We think we see, but don't see clearly. We think we are sure, yet get confused. We make errors of judgment at twilight.

A Rabbi asked his disciples, "When do you know it is morning?"

"It is when you can distinguish a fig tree from an olive tree", said a student.

The teacher was not satisfied. He asked another student.

"It is when you can see the difference between a sheep and a dog."

Still not getting the right answer the teacher said, "It is when you can recognise the person coming to you as a brother or sister."

In the biblical language about the day and the night we are not referring to our usual day and night. It is about the moral and spiritual quality of light or its absence that the Scripture refers to. Most crimes are committed at night. So, criminal tendency is identified with darkness. Most of those who want to do wrong things do it under cover. They do not want to come to light, to be exposed.

Christ came as light in a world of darkness and death. The gospels reflect the prophecy of Isaiah who said:

> "The people who were sitting in darkness saw a great light; those who were sitting in the land and shadow of death, upon them a light dawned." Matthew 4:16; Isaiah 9:2

This was the beginning of the enlightening gospel of Christ. Early Christians took this light into their conduct and way of life. The truthfulness and transparency of their daily living and their relationship to others were well-known. One could distinguish Christians from others by the way they talked and dealt with others. They were mostly ordinary people or even those below the poverty line. Yet they believed that they were children of light and that they belonged to a different order of society where the darkness of evil had no power.

In the morning, we wash ourselves, change our clothes, and put on what is necessary for our day-time work. We no longer wear the night dress. Our conduct is open to the daylight. We are to shed off the ways of evil as we change dirty clothes.

Yet it is difficult for many in the world since the twilight lingers with its confusing shadows and erroneous perceptions. We are unable to see a brother in a man who works for us, or a sister in a young woman who passes by. We abuse, attack, harass, rape, kill... then it is not yet morning.

Lent is the break of dawn when we make an effort to see clearly what is what and who is who. We struggle, yet we do it with the power of the Holy Spirit who discerns everything. Jesus our Lord also struggled in the desert fighting the powerful enemy, but he won. So we hold on to the hand of our Lord as we make this Lenten journey from darkness.

Day Nineteen

The Return

> "Therefore the Lord God sent him forth from the garden of Eden, to till the ground from which he was taken. He drove out the man; and at the east of the garden of Eden he placed the cherubim, and a sword flaming and turning to guard the way to the tree of life."
> Genesis 3: 23-24

Suppose by some unfortunate turn of events a certain man's house is confiscated. He and his family are being driven out of the home they loved and where they lived happily for many years. It is quite likely that on their way they would turn around and have a last desperate look before the house disappears from the view.

Adam and Eve were in the same position. They fell from grace, and consequently they were driven out of the blessed state of paradise, the garden of Eden. They must have turned around with broken hearts to glance at their lost home. While living on earth, they continued to harbour in their hearts a deeply painful homesickness throughout their life. Humanity inherited this state as it now lives in exile on earth.

We are all spiritually homesick. We find that our present reality, marked by disease, pain, suffering and death, does not give us as much joy and contentment as was given to our first parents in

The Fast and the Feast

paradise. We deeply long to return our true home -a certain *ghar wapsi*[1] in the best sense of the term, far above the narrow loyalties to one religion or other.

In the Orthodox tradition we turn to the east in our public prayers and liturgy. It symbolically expresses our deep spiritual longing to return to paradise. We have a great sunrise too in the east. Jesus Christ our Saviour, "the sun of justice", has opened the gate of paradise, the way to the tree of life, where an angel had been posted, armed with a flaming, revolving sword to prohibit any re-entry.

The Lenten prayers repeatedly refer to the story of Adam and Eve losing the paradise. They also express the firm faith and hope that through our suffering in this world, through ascetic practices of fasting and constant prayer, and through mutual forgiveness and acts of compassion, on the model of Christ, the Holy Spirit will enable us to return to the house of our heavenly Father. So the painful forty days need to be considered as part of an intense preparation for our happy "home-coming". In the context of the parable of the woman who lost and found her coin Jesus said:

> "In the same way, I tell you, there is joy in the presence of the angels of God over one sinner who repents."   Luke 15:10

---

[1] Hindi word meaning "home-coming". The word "ghar" is of Sanskrit origin meaning "home" and "wapsi" is of Persian origin, meaning "coming back". The term has been applied to a series of religious conversion activities facilitated by certain Indian Hindu organisations.

Day Twenty

The Instrument

On the third Sunday of the Lent, after the Holy Qurbana, when I was about to leave the sanctuary, one of the altar boys brought to me a small bundle of ball pens. He requested me to bless them on the altar because his exams were to start that week. Upon my enquiring about who owned those pens he said they were some ten boys and girls who waited outside the church. Slightly amused by the 'instrumental' faith of those young students I invited them all to assemble inside the church and had a friendly chat. To my question, 'Who writes the exam, you or your pen?', their answer was a shy, suppressed smile. They put aside their pens, and we had a special prayer for strength and blessings, as they appeared to be rather stressed about the impending exams.

We deal with all sorts of instruments every day. But there is a difference between living human beings who are created in God's image and the various instruments we use as means to fulfill our daily needs of food, clothing, shelter, transportation, communication, learning, entertainment and so on. We human beings are supposed to be masters of the instruments that we design and fabricate, not the other way round as it happens so often today in our technology-dominated society.

We are God's children, not instruments, though we are to carry out the will of God in this world. We are not pre-programmed robots, however efficient and endowed with artificial intelligence they are, but beings with freedom and creativity gifted to us by our Creator.

Jesus was vehemently critical of the public demonstration of fasting, prayer and other expressions of piety and charity. Many people in his time considered them to be instruments with saving power.

Lent is a time for us to discern the key difference between instruments we use and the human persons we are. Unless we undergo the process of conversion and become new human persons there is no value in the precision and efficacy of instruments we fashion. They might most likely turn against us as deadly weapons like in nuclear and missile technology, in chemical and bacterial warfare etc.

> "I tell you that unless your righteousness surpasses that of the scribes and the Pharisees, you will not enter the kingdom of God."   Matthew 5:20

Day Twenty-one

The Argumentation

C an we argue with God? Most of us may not be confident enough to answer that question. Some of us may find it irrelevant. Some others may consider it blasphemous. How can we puny human beings argue with our Creator God?

Perhaps we have the popular negative notion that arguing signifies rebellion and disobedience. But arguing can be a creative dialogue. In such cases it is a committed conversation between two dedicated individuals or groups with logical clarity and consideration of all the consequences of the point in question, with a clear view of the ultimate goal. Well-known Indian economist and Nobel Laureate Amartya Sen has a beautiful book, 'The Argumentative Indian'. He brings out the ancient Indian tradition where both men and women participate in creative argumentation in public on philosophical and social questions.

In the gospels we see at least two women arguing with Christ: the Samaritan woman and the Syro-Phoenician woman. Interestingly enough both are considered by mainstream Jews as outcasts, (a sort of *mleccha*, as the high caste Hindus once called the outsiders to their caste) with whom respectable Jews should not have any social interaction.

On the fourth Sunday of Lent we have read the incident of the Syro-Phoenician woman pleading with Jesus for the healing of her daughter. Jesus raises objections to her request, saying that he was sent only to the people of Israel and not to the outsiders. He even refers to his people the Jews as "master" in comparison to the others for whom he used the term "dogs". Not being intimidated or offended by the rather humiliating answer of Jesus, the woman responds with logic and perseverance. Finally Jesus is beaten by this courageous woman, until then a total stranger to him. He recognised the power of her faith and argument, and praised her:

"Woman, great is your faith." Matthew 15:28

What a compliment! He immediately assured her that her daughter was healed. The objections that Jesus raised were in fact the usual objections of those Jews who had a very narrow, racist and exclusivist notion of the Messiah. He raised these objections in public in order to teach them a lesson that it was not the race or caste or the claim to be the people of God that counted, but firm faith and the willingness to receive God's grace and healing. The life-giving gospel is open to all who believe, and Christians do not constitute a special caste. This notion of exclusivity is a misconception that ancient St Thomas Christians in India have held to a large extent down the centuries.

Day Twenty-two

The Siddhi

"Who is this? Even the wind and the waves obey Him!"

Mark 4:41

Lenten prayers repeatedly highlight great heroes in the Old Testament like Moses and Elijah, Joshua and Daniel, Hananiah (Shadrach) and his two friends as examples of persons who accomplished superhuman feats as a result of fasting and prayer. Moses could ascend the mountain of God and receive the Ten Commandments. Elijah could stop the rain or bring down fire from heaven or ascend to heaven in a fiery chariot. Joshua could stop the sun and the moon in their course. Daniel could shut the mouth of lions in the den where he was thrown to be torn apart. Hananiah (Shadrach) and his two friends came out whole and unhurt from the intensely heated furnace. We learn that the elemental forces of nature are brought under their control, and that is what we call their miraculous powers (Exodus 19; Joshua 10:12-13; I Kings 17-19; II Kings 2:8; Daniel 3; 6:10-18).

When we read the biblical passages referring to these heroes, we may notice two things:

First, we come to recognize the intensity of their commitment and the prophetic zeal with which they pursued their vision, how they purified themselves from all selfish goals for the sake of a great cause. This is the essence of fasting. It is not simply abstaining from food, drink, sex and other externals, but positively and single-mindedly pursuing the path of justice and truth for the common good. They did not compromise on the great principles, but stood against both the royal power and populist notions of power at great risk of their own lives. Second, they were able to stand above the ordinary, first of all by strictly bringing under their control all their senses connected to the fundamental human drives of hunger, thirst, sex, power, fame, authority and so on. This is the essential frame of fasting. Jesus followed it in his fasting and prayer in the desert, in the encounter with the Satan. Third, the power of mastery over elemental forces of nature like water, fire, air, earth's gravitational pull, movement of stars, planets and the like arose from the basic control of their own self. So it is not simply miraculous, but a logical consequence of their determined mastery over themselves. In India we would call it *siddhi,* the extraordinary ability to perform feats of great power. Anyone can acquire such powers provided one is able to follow the arduous path to control one's senses. In the Christian tradition, though we respect the *siddhi* of ascetics, we are taught by the example of Jesus not to use it or advertise it for our selfish interests for wealth, pleasure and fame. It is meant only for healing and reconciliation, for justice and peace, and thus to witness to God's deep compassion, forgiveness and care for us human beings and all God's creation. *Siddhi* is of no spiritual value without deep love.

Day Twenty-three

The Centering

The ancient medical symbol of a snake entwining a vertical rod is familiar to us. Used still in the modern medical profession in different forms it is given various interpretations. In one version it is referred to as the symbol of the Greek god Asclepius, the god of healing and renewal of life. Since a snake periodically sloughs off its outer body layer, it is said to represent renewal and return to youthful life. It is also an ambiguous symbol since the physicians and their medicines remain in between life and death; they can either heal or kill.

It is remarkable that in the Book of Numbers a similar symbolism is associated with the brazen serpent raised by Moses in the middle of the camp of Israelites for the healing of those bitten by poisonous snakes (Numbers 21:9). It was a curse against those who rebelled against God during their forty years of wandering in the desert. The very symbol of curse became the symbol of healing. This is further taken up by Christ, the heavenly physician, in his incarnate life:

> "As for me, if I am lifted up from the earth, I will draw all people to myself."   John 12:32

"Just as Moses lifted up the snake in the wilderness, so the son of Man will be lifted up."   John 3:14

In the Orthodox Syriac liturgical tradition we symbolically enact this saying of Christ by erecting a wooden cross on a raised wooden stand in the middle of the nave of the church on mid-Lent Wednesday. As the people of Israel bitten by poisonous snakes looked up to the brazen serpent and were healed, we look up to Christ on the cross for healing and protection from evil and the death of sin.

The centre of the church representing Space, and the midpoint of the Lent representing Time are significant. They stand for our life span and the space of the universe. So the life-giving Cross of Christ, the Tree of Life that heals nations, is planted at the very centre of Space and Time.

Every believer who enters the church is instructed to kiss the red trapping of the cross in repentance and hope. We need to take this symbol of the Cross of Christ, our Healer-Saviour, to our heart, the innermost core of our existence.

When in danger human beings usually look outside for any help. When we are about to drown we desperately stretch out our hands and look out for something to hold on to. But in our spiritual life we will come to a point where we cannot find anything or anybody from outside to come and help us. All that we depend on, or put our trust in, will vanish. In the thick darkness we will grope around for outer light, but we have only the inner light to enlighten us. Therefore we need to implant the cross in our heart so that we can draw healing and life from this inexhaustible inner fountain, the very source of our being.

In the Lenten period we make a special effort to weave our life round the cross of Christ, and search for the inner light of Jesus amidst the surrounding darkness of suffering and hopelessness. We cannot by any means ignore the suffering of people, those who crave for a touch of healing, and those who dwell in the dark shadows of death. Lifting up the cross of Christ that radiates healing and hope, light and life is the holy task that we take up these days.

The Fast and the Feast

Day Twenty-four

The Intercessor

In the Lenten Friday midnight prayers, we are exhorted thus:

> "Take courage, O you who pray; do not be dispirited or slothful, because the entire prayer of the Son of God is for you. Therefore, attach your prayer to his powerful prayer, and then your prayer will be answered."

What a consolation for those who have feelings of despair while they pray! It often happens that we feel helpless and confused in our prayers. We are not sure if our prayers will be answered. We need some degree of certainty about the result of our prayers. But then we need to know how to pray. The admonition cited above teaches us a method or "technique" of prayer. We need to attach our prayers to the great high-priestly prayer of our Lord Jesus Christ in our favour. We are used to sending "attachments" along with our letters and email messages. If there is an attachment it is indicated by a special sign. The attachment goes only together with the main message.

Christ is our unique intercessor before God, the Father. He is the only mediator between God and the humanity. According to the Letter to the Hebrews, Christ is our pioneer in faith, our eternal high priest, our mediator and intercessor.

"He is able to save completely those who come to God through him, because he always lives to intercede for them."

Hebrews 7:25

According to St Gregory the Theologian (4th century), Jesus Christ, the Second Person of the Trinity, "still pleads for us as Man" with his full humanity which is united with the Word of God incarnate.

"For there is one God and one mediator between God and human kind, the man Christ Jesus."   1 Timothy 2:5

We invoke the Holy Virgin, Mother of God and other saints to pray for us. This is fully in tune with the unique intercession of Jesus Christ. The Holy Mother, the apostles and the saints cannot make any prayer apart from the prayer of Christ our High Priest, for they themselves have received the grace and holiness of God through Christ the only Mediator. In holiness and by the practice of virtue they are fully integrated to Christ. As we ask others to pray for us in this world, so we ask the Holy Virgin and the saints, who overcame the world by the power of the Holy Spirit, to pray for us through Jesus Christ, our Saviour. We pray for them too. Praying for them and requesting their prayers is the great sign of our communion with those who are fully in communion with our Lord. Their prayers for us are also attached to the prayer of the Lord, and are more powerful than the prayers of those who still struggle in this sinful world.

The Church teaches us that our prayers are not to be isolated individual supplications but collective outpouring of the heart of the whole people of God. It is compared to the image of the rain. Rain falls drop by drop. Each drop of water by itself has no power. But when tens of thousands of drops are collected, they become a mighty stream. It is hardly possible for us to stop such a formidable torrent of water. Our prayer in community is likened to such a powerful current of water that can break open the door of divine mercy.

In the Lenten period, we are admonished to add each drop of our prayer to the prayers of all those who pray unceasingly for us and for the world. Above all it is our Lord Jesus Christ who prays for us. So let us take courage and persist in our prayer without any doubt or disappointment.

Day Twenty-five

The Breath

"Let everything that breathes praise the Lord."   Psalm 150:6

O f all ancient civilizations of the world, India alone seems to have gone deep into the mystery of human breathing in order to connect it with spirituality. The Yogic understanding and practice of "*Pranayama*"[1] begins with simple breathing exercises, enters the field of vital energy and finally leads on to higher states of consciousness. Here our usual breathing is controlled in such a way as to create new levels of spiritual awareness.

Breathing is life, and it comes to us naturally from the moment of our birth to the moment when we breathe our last. The Jewish-Christian Scripture, in fact, begins the story of creation with the Spirit (=breath, wind) of God breathing over the dark and the deep, sweeping over the face of the waters of nothingness (Genesis 1:1-2).

> "Then the Lord God formed man from the dust of the ground, and breathed into his nostrils the breath of life; and the man became a living being."   Genesis 2:7

---

[1] The formal practice of controlling the breath.

It is in continuation of this that in the New Testament, with the coming of Christ, the Holy Spirit or the Holy Breath of God, is associated with the new creation, the renewal of all created reality. The Church is the icon of the new humanity formed by the Holy Spirit beginning with the Pentecost experience as promised by Christ.

The breath of life in us is of divine origin. It is one of the most profound mysteries that we daily live with without being aware of it. But we can explore it as much as we are able as it has been done in this country.

We have a common problem of bad breath when food particles degenerate between our teeth, or when we have certain diseases. Even simple abstaining from all food and drink can create bad breath. We are daily bombarded with all kinds of pharmaceutical remedies for bad breath! When we eat food gluttonously without gratitude to any one, when we breathe out abusive words against others, when we harbour evil thoughts and jealousy, when we pollute the atmosphere with all kinds of chemical and industrial waste, our breath is poisoned. It degenerates, and it is the end of life. It smells of death -the ultimate bad breath.

It is interesting to know that the Christian tradition speaks of the "sweet breath" of saintly persons who have transformed their human breath as a continuation of the breath of God through their holy lives. This is not only metaphorical but also experiential. One of the Sedra prayers in the liturgy make us pray:

> "May our breath be filled with Your fragrance, our mouths be opened to sing Your praise and our tongues made ready to sing Your hymns."   (Mor Osthathios of Antioch)

Lent is the time to learn to sweeten our breath by the practice of virtues. Those of us who are specially gifted and called by God in monasteries or elsewhere may also try to develop a practical

Lenten *Pranayama* with the goal of attuning our breathing to the rhythm of the Holy Spirit and of producing ever higher states of awareness of love, compassion and the presence of God.

The Fast and the Feast

Day Twenty-six

The Thooyobo

The Eucharistic liturgy begins with what is called the service of "Thooyobo" (preparation). This touching preparatory part of the liturgy is performed nowadays by the priest alone in the silence and seclusion of the closed sanctuary, while the congregation sings the morning office outside of it. It is done silently or in subdued voice and the whole preparation becomes the proper base for the public liturgy.

The preparatory service comprises, among other things, these elements:

Placing of bread and wine to be consecrated on the altar.
Prayers of personal repentance and confession of the priest
Priest's prayerful vesting or wearing of sacred vestments,
Intercessory prayers for all kinds of people from Adam and
Eve to the present.

For those who do it in its true spirit it is really empowering and deeply moving. We may take this "thooyobo" (preparation) for the public liturgy as a metaphor for other aspects of our spiritual life too. For example, the Lent is considered as preparatory to the great and saving celebration of the death and resurrection of Christ.

Closeted in the silent cave of our Lenten practice, we may experience dimensions of silence, sobriety and sojourn essential for our Lenten spirituality. We do not need to display our fasting and related practices to people outside though we join the community prayers and observe the fasting rules of the Church in parishes, monasteries, seminaries and homes.

The metaphor of preparation can also be applied to our whole life. As the ascetic Fathers point out again and again, our whole life in this world is preparatory for the eternal life to come. We try to bring out the holiness of life through meditation of the Word of God and the exercise of virtues.

Let us enter the secret chamber of our heart as Jesus taught us. In repentance and hope let us place our lives on the altar of Christ as a living sacrifice of praise; let us put on the "garment of incorruption", the vestment of immortal glory. Let us uphold all those who are weak and suffering, the poor and the oppressed before the merciful Father in heaven.

Day Twenty-seven

The Wings

Human beings are winged creatures! Or so they dream to be. From the time of the Wright brothers in the late 19th century to that of space shuttles and the solar powered experimental airplane now flying around the globe, humanity has been perfecting the art of flying. Religious mythology is replete with flying beings and even airplanes like our puranic "Pushpaka Vimana".

The Christian tradition, however, has always held that the soul has wings and is capable of rising to the heavenly heights. We are taught that the soul is weightless, invisible and unaffected by the power of gravity. It is probably this spiritual soul-force within us that make us resolute flight-aspirants.

> "Those who wait on the Lord will renew their strength; they will soar on wings like eagles."   Isaiah 40:31

The Lenten prayers describe prayer as having wings.

> "Prayer is love-ful: unless love lifts it up its wings are weak".

The ascetics and people who genuinely observe fasting witness to the body's light-weight experience. In other words, the soul's character is transferred to the body which is naturally heavy and pulled down by the earth's gravity. There is a phenomenon of 'levitation', the gift of rising gently from the ground while in prayer or meditation attested to by certain spiritual figures. We are not focusing here on the physical rising but simply mention that even that is reportedly possible. We are concerned about the lifting up of our inner person to the heights of a new awareness of our spiritual gifts through fasting and prayer.

Interpreting the experience of Adam and Eve in paradise before the fall and on earth after the fall, the Fathers like St Gregory of Nyssa would say that the physical body of our first parents, which was weightless and transparent in paradise, became heavy, opaque and thus subject to the forces of nature on earth. So the spiritual struggle of humanity has always been to overcome this slavery of the body to the material forces, and to rise to its original transparency and lightness. In the observation of fasting and prayer and other spiritual exercises, we make an attempt to subordinate the instinctual natural drives like hunger, thirst and sex to our higher goals of spiritual soaring and transcendence. We also need to be liberated from our inclination to debasing passions like power, pleasure, possessiveness, and aggressiveness.

So spiritual exercises like fasting and prayer need to develop wings in order to climb high levels of experience. According to the best of the Gospel tradition, love alone generates those wings.

The Fast and the Feast

Day Twenty-eight

The Waiting

We were a small motley crowd huddled in the waiting room of a famous physician in a big Kerala hospital. Coming from different places we hardly knew each other. Since the rule was first-come-first-served we had taken our seats already by 7.30 in the morning though the doctor would come only by 10.30.

Breaking the initial silence people started talking. One gentleman in a wheelchair said he was brought back to life by the doctor from a usually fatal condition. Some others also gave testimonies for the compassion and competence of the physician. Being a first-timer to consult that doctor I was given a lot of advice by experienced fellow patients, but all pointed to the possibility of healing. In fact, our discussion was centred on hope, healing and the skill of the physician.

Being in the time of the great Lent, I happened to draw an analogy between the doctor's waiting room and the Lenten period. I was reminded of the daily prayers in which we repeatedly meditate on disease and suffering, healing and the heavenly physician. In the prayers from the Orthodox tradition, sin is the disease and ill-health is the suffering that results as a consequence of sin. The uprooting of sin along with its symptoms constitutes the process of healing while Jesus Christ is the physician and compassionate healer.

We had come to the Lenten waiting room with various diseases of body, mind and soul. We were strangers to each other. But we broke into an animated conversation, focused on each other's disease, its symptoms and the suffering it caused. Each disease was different. Yet we were united in our deep desire for healing and the hope that this desire would be fulfilled by our able and sympathetic physician. We listened to each other with understanding, because we were all more or less in the same condition of illness. We supported and encouraged each other and became one body in the intense and shared desire for healing and wholeness.

Is it not what is expected of the church community as we observe the Lent? Let us pray for each other. Let us be sympathetic to each other's faults and shortcomings. May we encourage each other to wait patiently for our Healer in faith and hope. Our Physician is the one who takes up our pain and bears our suffering.

> "When evening came, they brought to him many who were demon-possessed; and He cast out the spirits with a word and healed all who were ill. This was to fulfill what was spoken through Isaiah the prophet: he himself took our infirmities and carried away our diseases." Matthew 8:17

The Fast and the Feast

Day Twenty-nine

The Owning

The Sanskrit word "tiryak" stands for all non-human creatures in general. The word means bent, horizontal, slanted or crooked, and it refers particularly to animals that walk on four legs. Their spine is horizontal to the ground and the face and eyes directed to the earth. This contrasts with the straight body of a human being who can stand erect and look up to the sky ("homo erectus" marks a crucial mile stone in the story of biological evolution).

The bent woman whom Jesus heals in the synagogue on a Sabbath day had been physically reduced to the animal condition. She had put up with suffering, with the indifference and contempt of others, for over 18 years. She had never dreamt that her condition would be altered, and so never sought any healing. Jesus, therefore, had to call her to come forward, and he placed his hands on her to restore the original condition of her body. This is one of those few occasions when Jesus heals someone without an explicit request to be healed.

Jesus' act of liberating this old woman, probably a poor widow, on the margins of society, provoked an indignant reaction on the part of the leader of the Synagogue. He deplored it and decreed that the act of healing was a "work" that violated the holy Sabbath of the Lord. Sharply retorting, Jesus referred to the animal condition by asking if the owners of cattle took care to water their oxen and donkeys even on a Sabbath day. Then Jesus conferred a great honour on that insignificant woman reduced to animal condition by her physical infirmity and social apathy. He called her "the daughter of Abraham". By raising a poor anonymous woman practically ignored by all to a new name and status, Jesus owned her as a true descendant of Abraham.

Jesus thus once again illustrated the Gospel of the kingdom. He highlights for us the calling of the Church today to own the disinherited, to straighten those who are stooping and languishing in the shadow of death and gather all those in the margins into a new race of human beings. Jesus Christ is our redeemer and liberator says:

> "Come to me, all who are weary and heavy-laden, I will give you rest."   Matthew 11:28

The Fast and the Feast

Day Thirty

The Martyrs

he world was terribly shocked when the ISIS (Islamic State) army brutally beheaded 21 young Coptic Orthodox Christian workers in Libya recently. They were killed because they were Christians. They did not do any harm to anyone. They left their poor villages in southern Egypt in search of work in order to help their families survive. In the video clip telecast by the assassins, some of those victims were seen to be reciting the name of Jesus moments before their innocent blood mingled with the waters of the Mediterranean just "south of Rome".

Contrary to all human logic, amazing divine grace, forgiveness and faith prevailed in the families of those young men who died as bold witnesses (martyrs) to their crucified Lord. The mother of the two young brothers, Bishoy and Stefanos, killed along with 19 others, thanked the IS army for letting her beloved children enter the kingdom of God by the gate of martyrdom! There were originally only 20 Coptic Orthodox Christians. The 21st one was a young black African from Chad who, watching the amazing faith of his fellow workers, confessed Christ and was beheaded as a martyr.

The Coptic Orthodox Church has declared the 21 youth as martyrs for Christ and recognized February 15 as the Feast day of their commemoration in the Church calendar. One is reminded of the 40 martyrs of Sebaste brutally killed by the Roman army of Emperor Licinius in Armenia in 320 AD. They were young soldiers who refused to renounce their Christian faith, and were thrown naked into a frozen lake. We remember their martyrdom on the fifth Saturday of the great Lent. Their story is touchingly similar to that of the Coptic Christians. In the Sebaste killings in the 4th century there was also a courageous mother who stood by her son encouraging him to face the cruel death with unswerving faith and hope in Christ. There was also one young man among the 40 who, unable to face torture and death, left his brothers for the warm bath kept ready for anyone who renounced his faith. But a Roman guard, watching the courage of faith of the 39 young men, confessed Christ, jumped into the frozen lake and courted the death of a martyr!

The Sedra prayer for the Feast of the 40 Martyrs of Sebaste in the Lent says that the number 40 of the martyrs suits well the 40 Lenten days of the Lord's fasting and prayer. What can we say about the number 21 of our contemporary Coptic martyrs? Can we say the number 21 stands for 21st century? Yes, probably. Christian faith is going to face great suffering in this century. It has started in many places including our own beloved motherland India. What would then be our witness to the Prince of Peace and the Gospel of love? (the Greek word 'martyria', cognate of martyr, is translated as 'witness').

> "Then they will deliver you to tribulation, and will kill you, and you will be hated by all nations because of my name... But the one who endures to the end will be saved." Matthew 24:9-13

Day Thirty-one

The Light

"The people who were sitting in darkness saw a great light,
and those who were sitting in the land and shadow of death,
upon them a light dawned."   (Matthew 4:16; Isaiah 9:2)

Suppose you are stranded in a strange and deserted place in the thick of night with no sense of direction or light or help. A normal human person is likely to panic. This can happen even in a lift that gets stuck with all lights off in a well-peopled building. Deep fear can grip you. Terror-stricken, some weak-hearted persons may even succumb to death.

Darkness casts the shadow of death. "To live in the region and shadow of death" is the most painful experience for human beings. A little glimmer of light, even very far, can bring hope and life to such people.

"Let there be light" was the first Word of God according to the Bible (Genesis 1:3). Light was the very first creation of God.

When Jesus first appeared publicly in Galilee to announce the Good News of the kingdom God, He came as light for all those who lived in the land and shadow of death. A great prophecy was being fulfilled.

We know that light is the source of life on our earth. If there is no sunlight there will not be any green vegetation on earth. If there is no green vegetation all human and animal life will suddenly disappear from the face of the earth.

This is so in the spiritual life as well. Jesus Christ is our light as we grope in the dark. Christian faith is a faith of light and life. If we do not expose ourselves to the light of Christ, our spiritual life will soon be extinct. Terrifying darkness will overwhelm us.

An important synonym for baptism in the Greek language is "photisma" or enlightenment. In baptism a child is brought to the light of Christ, and is enlightened. So the child is born again to a new life - from the merely biological life to the spiritual life.

We are all born again. That is something that we tend to forget. We forget our origin. We do not see the light of Christ. We do not like to live in the light of Christ. Without getting any reminder or follow up of that great new birth, without paying any attention to the ethical standards required of that new birth, some people seek to be born again and again. One re-birth, one baptism, is the ancient rule of the church. Let us not violate that rule. But internally we should continually be born again and again, always a new creation in Christ Jesus our Lord.

Lent for many may be a shadowy period because of its strict rules of fasting and abstinence. But as we walk in the shadow of death in this world symbolized by the Lenten time, we continually seek and meditate on the dawn of light, the only source of our life.

> "You are all children of the light and children of the day. We do not belong to the night or to the darkness."
>
> I Thessalonians 5:5

The Fast and the Feast

Day Thirty-two

The Lamp

It is a familiar sight in Hindu temple festivals in India where traditionally dressed women wait with lighted oil lamps to receive the image of a god or goddess taken out in procession. A similar reception by young girls with flowers sometimes takes place when important personalities are received at social functions. It happens not infrequently that the arrival of the personalities gets delayed, and some of the waiting young girls get tired, faint or become sleepy and lose their lamps and flowers. This reminds us of the well-known parable of the Ten Virgins told by Jesus (Matthew 25:1-13). It is one of the favourite Lenten themes. Christian art especially in the West is deeply influenced by this parable of great aesthetic and spiritual significance.

The contrast between the vigilant preparedness of the five wise virgins and the lazy sleepiness of the five foolish virgins illustrates the contrast between those who eagerly wait for the Lord and those who are indifferent to the goal of life. The parable clearly points to the end of history and the end of our life when we face the final judgment of God.

> "Therefore keep watch, because you do not know the day or the hour." Matthew 25:13

The Lent is symbolically the span of our life which is a time of vigilance and readiness to receive the bridegroom, and enter the chamber of lights with him to participate in the everlasting wedding celebration. The vigil, the state of wakefulness, is an essential part of Lenten fasting. This does not always mean that we literally deprive ourselves of sleep, but that we take care of our internal awareness with a view to enlightenment. Continuous prayers like the "Jesus Prayer" with breathing and the regular reading and meditation of the Word of God can help us trim and illuminate our awareness.

Above all the Lent is a time of joyful expectation. We are filled with hope for the future, and therefore we do not count time. But imagine the contrary experience of looking at future with a dismal anxiety . Usually this is our lot. We count time; we are bored; we pay all our attention to trivial things and silly conversation. We are disappointed, and we quarrel at home and in society. When something important happens we are not there. We regret, but it is too late.

In one of the Lenten prayers we pray:

> "Re-lighten, O Lord, our lamps that are extinguished for want of righteousness."

This is about the equipment that we are required to carry with us as we wait. Christianity brought to the world a very fine set of ethical standards in social life- justice, equality, freedom, human dignity, peacefulness, forgiveness, honesty, humility, service-mindedness. These values constitute the oil that keeps the light of our hope burning. But now regrettably most Christians have lost these essential ethical standards of right living. The Christian mission now is to restore these essential values required for a really human community life.

All our socio-political ills like rampant corruption and denial of justice to the poor arise from our lack of will or indifference to practise them. So we need to check and re-check if our lamps are still burning, if our dresses are smartly in order, if we are just and honest, humble and ready to serve our fellow human beings in need whatever be their race and religion.

Day Thirty-three

The Kanikonna

Jesus said:

> "The kingdom of God is like a man who casts seed upon the soil; and he goes to bed at night and gets up by day, and the seed sprouts and grows - how, he himself does not know. The soil produces crops by itself; first the blade, then the head, then the mature grain in the head."   Mark 4:26-28

I fondly remember the "Kanikonna" tree that stood on the northern side of the Old Seminary chapel and blossomed in March- April during the Lent season. (The tree is called Golden Shower Tree in English or scientifically *Cassia Fistula*. Its flower is the state flower of Kerala and the "auspicious-sight" flower of the Vishu festival, the time of Spring Equinox in South India). Every time we students walked into the chapel for the Lenten fasting Prayer of the Hours in the oppressive heat and humidity of South Indian summer, this modest tree with its rich golden yellow flowers was an enchanting and soothing sight. Every little branch was covered with bunches of flowers and on every bunch there would be some golden flowers in full bloom and dozens of green buds of various sizes, from the very big to the tiniest, waiting for their turn to bloom. Every bud patiently underwent the process of slow maturing. Every day there would be new flowers added to the older ones on hundreds of bunches, and towards the end of the Lent the whole tree would be only flowers and turn radiant with a golden hue. What was interesting was the efflorescence, the slow growth and gradual unfolding of the buds to full bloom.

Our Lenten spirituality, it seemed, was very much nourished by the flowering process of the Kanikonna. It was slow and steady. Every bud needed its own time to mature and unfold. Every step was taken slowly and gradually. There was no hurry, no space for despair. Every day new blooms appeared. Every bud comes out with a new message of hope -for the life, the beauty and the joy of the world.

The Orthodox spiritual tradition emphasizes the gradual steps like in the "Ladder of Spiritual Ascent" of St John Climacus. The 40 days of fasting and prayer of Jesus in the desert, the 40 days of Moses climbing the Mount Sinai in the desert, and the 40 days of the prophet Elijah walking in the desert to Mount Horeb, all reveal this gradual character of our Lenten spiritual exercise. Nature's life cycles give us inspiring models for our own pilgrimage.

Day Thirty-four

The Tears

Tears are older than smiles in human biological evolution. They have a clear physical function. The lacrimal secretion known as tears constantly cleans and lubricates the eye balls. However, we usually associate tears with our emotions.

Our eyes can be watery for various reasons. Some of the reasons are physical. For example, when we have an allergy or nerve malfunction, when dust particles or other irritants enter the eye in response to some pungent vapour like that of the onion, we 'cry'.

At the psychological level, tears are related to our deep emotions. For example, when we have a sense of loss by death or otherwise of a family member or a close friend, or when we lose some of our valuable material belongings by theft, fire or accident.

Some cry by empathy, when they see the pain and misery of another person, or read the news of a tragic event involving death and suffering of people. Some of us cry when we are afraid, or feel insulted or helpless and so on. These are tears of sadness. Some shed tears when they are overcome with a sudden burst of joy that is unexpected. This happens, for example, when they achieve a coveted position or prize or a bumper lottery, when there is a chance meeting with a long-lost bosom friend or when they hear a touching word of appreciation. These are tears of joy.

Regardless of the emotional trigger, through the shedding of tears, we are able to release the mounting stress in us, restore the balance, and clean the windscreen of our mind, just like the physical function of tears that lubricate and thus clean the eyes.

In the Lenten period the hymns and prayers speak a great deal about tears, but on a different plane. First there are tears of repentance. We cry when we realize that we have done some serious wrong to others by hurting them in some way, by neglecting our duties, squandering our resources, being insensitive to the love of others or when we feel remorse for some criminal acts on our part. At a psychological level or a deeper spiritual level, these tears are considered healthy. These are the tears that are associated with a true sacramental confession. Tears can be more or less a sure sign that the person realizes his or her serious sinful acts (not forgetting that some people can wilfully produce tears that are deceptive, the 'crocodile' tears). Repentance should not be limited to the admission of sins but also a sincere submission to the love, compassion and forgiveness of God, and consequently a wilful determination on our part not to repeat the sinful conduct. We tend to cry when we receive unconditional forgiveness for the sins of omission and commission on our part. This leads us to reconciliation with God and our fellow human beings. It generates internal peace and the virtue of genuine hope within us. We are assisted in this process by the grace of the Holy Spirit who helps us discern the way of light and life.

Secondly, there are tears that are generally called 'the gift of tears' in the spiritual tradition of the eastern church. This is far deeper than the tears of repentance. The physical, emotional and ordinary spiritual reasons are not there. These tears flow out of a person spontaneously without wilful knowledge or control when that person is filled with a profound awareness of God's creation, the mystery of love and the depth of existence. These tears embody all that we speak about regarding compassion, empathy, repentance, forgiveness, joy, reconciliation and so on, but transcend all these. Their source is totally unknown. So it is called a gift. It is ecstatic in character for those who receive this gift. The gift of tears points to the mystery of creation. The gospels pass under respectful silence the tears that flowed from Jesus in the solitary nights with only the moon and the stars, the wild figs and olives or the total darkness as his only witnesses when he withdrew from even his close disciples and went apart to pray. They, however, explicitly mention Jesus weeping at the tomb of his friend Lazarus or at the sight of the beauty of Solomon's temple of Jerusalem. We may understand in human terms the reasons for his tears on such occasions, but not the other.

We have examples, even that only partly known, of saints like Saint Isaac of Nineveh who spoke about the experience of the gift of tears. As a young boy this writer had heard stories from an elderly gentleman contemporary of Saint Mar Gregorios of Pampady, about the discreet and abundant tears of the ascetic bishop while the latter was a deacon. Retrospectively one wonders if those tears had anything to do with this gift.

The Fast and the Feast

Day Thirty-five

The Night

"David got up in the thick of the night in order to sing praises to the wonderful decrees of God, and he saw the amazing beauty of the moon and the stars decking the firmament of the sky, and he marvelled at their order".

The night is glorified in the Lenten prayers notwithstanding its ambiguous symbolism related to ignorance and evil. The Lent itself, despite its apparent dryness of fasting and abstinence, can become a night of spiritual streams and revelation of the higher knowledge of the beauty of God's ordering of creation. For those inclined to a meditative quiet there is no better time than the night. Covered by the dark veil and hidden from curious eyes and with most of her children put to sleep, mother nature goes into a deep meditation herself. So the best time and place for our own meditation is the lap of nature at night. The gospels tell us that Jesus left the crowd and even his close disciples in the evenings "and went up alone to the mountain to pray." There he had no man-made building to stay in, but it was plain nature open to the vast sky.

For most people the vision of the sky at night is more enchanting than that of the day. While the blinding light of the sun eclipses all stars in the day sky, they come out in their infinite numbers and delightfully illuminate the night sky in the absence of the sun. When things go against us, when we suffer from serious setbacks, loss or disease we say it is night for us. But the very night of disarray and despair can provide to us an exquisite vision of the universe in its broader and brighter dimensions. Meditating on this mystery of the night vision we will be filled with new hope and plans for the future. The night is spiritually the most creative time for a deeper perception of our life.

As a practical step we need to go out at some odd hour of the night and watch the starry sky in a meditative mood thinking of the incredible distances of the stars, the amazing rhythm and harmony of the planetary and galactic movements. Being aware of our own breathing we can listen to the music and feel the pulse of the universe, and be profoundly grateful to God our Creator for the very life in us.

The Fast and the Feast

Day Thirty-six

The Test

As children we used to be amused by the song of the Indian Cuckoo, popularly called "Achen Kompathu pakshi" or "Vishu pakshi" in Kerala. This was a rather shy bird that appeared in Kerala during March- April. It was not easily visible, but its song was loud and resounding. Children used to parody the rhyming sound of the bird in humorously absurd words like "achen kompathu, amma varampathu". Hence its name "achen kompathu". As children we would exercise our creative skills and compete against each other by inventing funny two-line parodies. Some of us associated the bird song with the exams as the Achen-kompath bird used to appear in the season when we were preparing for our school exams in March. Later we also linked it to the Lenten season. Retrospectively one sees both the exams and the lent as a kind of test. Jesus was tested by the tempter, and he passed the rigorous exams in the desert's desolation after a 40-day long test.

The Achen-kompath bird was also a sign bird. Suppose you are praying hard to God for an answer to some knotty personal questions, but you do not receive a response. You may become dispirited and confused. Then, according to some, this bird's song might give you a clue to the solution of your problem. A great man of God in our time, Metropolitan Geevarghese Mar Osthathios of blessed memory once told us an amusing story. Staying at the Bethany Ashram of the Malankara Orthodox Church as a young sub-deacon he was praying for divine guidance as to his vocation-whether he should become a celibate priest or a married priest. After several days of prayer and meditation he was still wavering without any clear answer from God. Disappointed, he was about to depart from the ashram. All of a sudden he heard the song of this bird in the thickly wooded environment of Bethany. An interpretation of the bird call spontaneously rhymed in his mind. "Ippo kettenda. Pattam kettikko"(Don't get married now. Get ordained !). You may believe it or not. But he followed the bird's message to the great blessing of Church and society as later history proved. God's will can be revealed to us in mysterious and totally unexpected ways in nature. Some sort of a theophany, manifestation of the divine!

Recently I was visiting the family of a good friend of mine. They were passing through a very distressing time as their ancestral home, a very fine old building, had been destroyed by fire. By the grace of God no one was physically hurt. As I was taking leave of the family after the pastoral visit, we heard two "Achen-kompath" birds, hiding at some good distance from each other, make the familiar resounding call. With the burned house in the background the bird's sound simply rhymed in my mind as "Kathipokkotte. Daivam Koottunde" (Let it burn out, God is with us). My friends were strong in faith and trusted God's providential care. They too, I believe, probably heard it in a similar consoling way.

The family was literally passing through a fiery test. Some sounds and sights in nature can be a timely message from heaven. In this context I dared to interpret this as a sign of assurance about God's empowering presence and care in our moment of testing.

> "Look at the birds of the air, they do not sow or reap or store away in barns, and yet our heavenly Father feeds them. Are you not much more valuable than those birds?"
>
> Matthew 6:26

The Fast and the Feast

Day Thirty-seven

The Incense

"Botafumeiro" is the giant 80 kilogram censer (*dhoopakutty*) in the Cathedral of Santiago de Compostela in Spain. It hangs from the roof of the huge cathedral and is swung by a team of special operators who, to me, look like Spanish "matadores", or bullfighters. Some 40 kilograms of incense and charcoal are fed into it for every performance that attracts big crowds. It sends out huge columns of smoke in striking configurations in the air. The sight of this was a stunning experience for a priest used to small, handy censers in the Indian Orthodox parish churches.

The use of incense in liturgical worship was common to both the western and the eastern Christian traditions. However, it has become almost a nominal practice in the west today while eastern Christianity still generously makes use of incense in worship. There is a rich biblical symbolism associated with the smoke of incense and its fragrance. When we burn certain spices like frankincense in public worship the sweet-smelling smoke that rises into air is considered, according to biblical symbolism, to be the rising prayer of the community.

> "And the smoke of the incense, with the prayers of the saints, went up before God out of the angel's hand." Revelation 8:4

The fragrance of our offerings is well pleasing to God according to the Old Testament scripture. We are also called the "aroma of Christ" by St Paul (2 Corinthians 2:15). In one of the Lenten prayers Jesus Christ is called:

> "the pure smoke of incense that pleases the One who sent him by his self-offering, delights the creation with his fragrance, gladdens his handiwork with his sweetness" (Palm Sunday Night, Ethro)

Our prayers are to transcend the world of daily living while their fragrance gladdens and heals the surroundings. It is like music. Prayer at its core is music. That is why we chant musically even prayers written in prose. We know that music has this celebrated quality of rising above the divisions, harmonising disparate and dislocated elements in our surroundings.

Typologically we may consider the Lent as a giant censer. Our virtuous thoughts and actions, our prayers and intercessions, pain and suffering, sighs and tears - we offer these like frankincense to the glowing embers of the Lenten censer. They are then mixed with the prayers of the saints of all ages and all places, and rise to God's throne of mercy.

We sing the Psalm in every evening prayer:

> "May my prayer be counted as incense before You; the lifting up of my hands as the evening sacrifice." Psalm 141:2

Day Thirty-eight

The Buds

In traditional Christian Churches in Kerala children show great enthusiasm in collecting an array of flowers and colourful leaves of plants to bring to church on Palm Sunday. They enjoy throwing up flowers in playful delight during the special service of Hosanna. The day is also marked by the beautiful sight of the tender leaves of coconut trees (kuruthola) blessed during the service and carried by all the faithful. The Malankara Orthodox Church, according to its new lectionary, celebrates Palm Sunday also as the day of children.

Jesus rejoiced in the singing of Hosannas by children during his entry to Jerusalem. It was the fulfilment of a great Messianic prophecy (Psalm 8:2).

> "But when the chief priests and scribes saw the wonderful things He had done, and the children who were shouting in the temple, 'Hosanna to the Son of David', they became indignant , and said to Him, 'Do you hear what these children are saying?'. And Jesus said to them, 'Yes; have you never read, 'Out of the mouths of infants and nursing babies you have prepared praise for yourself?'"   Matthew 21:15-16

The close connection between the small children on the one hand and the sprouting seedlings and buds on the other is obvious. Both represent the budding life. Both hold promises for the future and life's fruitfulness. Both witness to the hope of new life and the new order of the world to be brought about by the Messiah. Both have a certain transparency and loveliness of innocence that attract discerning people of good will.

It may seem paradoxical that a radically new vision for the world and for a new order of life sprouts in the most unlikely place, namely the desert. All the biblical heroes that we celebrate in the Lenten prayers had something to do with the desert or desert-like situations hostile to life. The dreary desert of the great Lent can become the fertile seed-bed for the budding life.

The Fast and the Feast

Day Thirty-nine

The Hospitality

While living in a tent in the wilderness Abraham received three travellers in his tent-house under the shade of an oak tree. They were total strangers to Abraham. His hospitality became legendary, and the incident narrated in Genesis 18 gave rise to interpretations of the doctrine of Trinity later in the Christian patristic era, and also to the celebrated icon of "Philoxenia" (hospitality, literally 'love of strangers') by the Russian iconographer Andre Rublev in the 14th century. The theme of hospitality has found a place in the reflections of contemporary philosophers like Jacques Derrida and Paul Ricoeur as well as in the political ethics of modern nation states.

We know from experience that the poor are more hospitable than the rich in general. That means that the virtue of hospitality does not necessarily depend on material resources that we possess. In the ancient monastic tradition, hospitality was a prime Christian virtue for the monks living in the desert with practically nothing to offer to the guests. St Benedict (6th century) in the west instructed in his Rules to consider every guest as Christ himself. (Remember the ancient Indian dictum "Atithi devo bhavah" - let the guest be god).

In Christ's self-offering through suffering and death out of love for us and for our salvation we see the supreme example of divine hospitality. It is in the desert of the nothingness of self-emptying (kenosis) that God receives us strangers and aliens into the divine household and the banquet of the kingdom.

The anonymous woman who anointed Jesus at the house of Simon the rich Pharisee (Matthew 26:6-13 and parallels) deeply understood this and responded to the divine hospitality by an unusual and 'extravagant' act of human hospitality. Jesus drew out the contrast between her and Simon. The nameless and despised woman extended her hospitality at a very inhospitable time and place while the hospitality shown by the rich host was superficial and tainted with hidden ulterior motives.

The woman exemplified the meaning of the overwhelming divine hospitality of the Son of Man who was about to die on the cross by her own overwhelming, evocative, and seemingly 'crazy' gesture of love. Jesus alone recognized it and said that she did it for his burial. What a marvellous moment of mutual recognition between the divine and the human! In all likelihood, the nameless woman must have followed Jesus up to Calvary and beyond. Think of the "fragrance that filled the whole house" (John 12:3). Consider how the story of this gesture continues to be told and retold across the ages in memory of her as an integral part of the entire Gospel narrative (Matthew 26:13).

There is a subtle connection between love, hospitality and complete self-giving. It may be a bit difficult for us to understand the suffering and death of Christ as part of God's hospitality towards the created world. But Jesus himself tells us that:

> "There is no greater love than to lay down one's life for one's friends." John 15:13

Voluntary suffering for the sake of love for others is the ultimate in hospitality. When you take into your household people who are total strangers and passers-by, people who are not related to you in any way, people who are in some dire need of help, you are making a silent commitment to ultimately lay down your life for them. Here hospitality is salvation in its rich meaning. To be hospitable means to be committed to save life.

The opposite of philoxenia or love of the stranger is "xenophobia", fear of the stranger. We are taught to hate the alien, to suspect the passers by, to mistrust and fear anyone who comes towards us. The irony of the age is that our world is now being ruled by high security systems and alerts claiming to save our life. At ever-rising cost of resources and relationships we actually curtail human freedom and rights, natural camaraderie and fruitful human exchanges in order to build devices of death in the name of safety and salvation. The long-term blessings and promises to humanity that true hospitality brings in, like in the case of Abraham and Sarah, are becoming more and more alien to us.

> "See what great love the Father has lavished on us, that we should be called the children of God. And that is what we are!"   1 John 3:1

Day Forty

The Rising

It may be a pure coincidence of nature. The vigorous Passion Fruit vine (*Passiflora edulis*) and the delicate Easter Lily plant in my backyard showed up side by side with their splendid flowers during these days of the Holy Week when we meditate on the passion and resurrection of Jesus.

It is said that some imaginative Spanish missionaries in Latin America saw several signs of the crucifixion of Jesus when they saw the tropical flower of this vine for the first time, such as the three nails, five wounds, the crown of thorns and the lance that pierced his side. Their impressions gave rise to the name, Passion flower, which has remained to this day.

What intrigued me was the way the two flowers appeared together-the Passion and the Easter, in my humble garden. In the liturgical theology of the Orthodox Church the two are inseparable. The saving event that we commemorate and celebrate this week comprises the suffering, death and resurrection of Christ. They are one single unfathomable mystery.

In the medieval western Church's theology and spirituality, a heavy emphasis was placed on the physical pain and suffering (passion) of Christ, and so the Resurrection of Christ was relegated to the margins. The trend continued to modern times, and much of western art, literature and theatre including the much-hyped recent Mel Gibson film "The Passion of the Christ" typically represents the medieval obsession with the gruesome and macabre physical suffering of Christ. This may explain why the medieval Latin missionaries could not see in the splendid tropical flower the image of the radiant sun symbolizing the risen Christ rather than the exclusive tokens of the passion of Christ!

In the East, however, the Resurrection of Christ takes centre stage apart from those Eastern churches that came under the colonial influence of Portuguese and Spanish missionaries. Things have changed in the west after the second Vatican Council. Orthodox iconography of crucifixion and resurrection that portrays the equanimous and serene image of the crucified Jesus overcoming the horror of death has begun to influence the west.

The liturgical tradition has kept the healthy balance. There is no glorious resurrection without suffering and death, and there is no meaningful suffering and death without the hope of resurrection. Following the apostolic witness we proclaim Christ crucified and risen.

> "For I delivered unto you first of all that which I also received, how Christ died for our sins according to the scriptures, and that He was buried, and that He rose again according to the scriptures.... If Christ has not been raised, our preaching is vain and your faith also is vain"   1 Corinthians 15;3, 4, 14

Deprived of its transcendent dimension of hope, human suffering becomes absurd. Belief in resurrection is the only way to redeem human pain from its blind meaninglessness and futility.

The 21st century so far seems to be a century of suffering for the Christian faith. The age of the triumphalist western Christianity of crusades and colonial conquests is over. The Christian east had begun to suffer much earlier. Churches in the Middle East region, the very cradle of Christianity, continue to be in the crucible of intense suffering and face the threat of total elimination. Christian martyrdom of the first centuries under severe persecution seems to be recurring under new oppressive forces in our age.

An Arab Christian friend Michel Nseir sent the following message:

> "In our turbulent part of the Arab world, still holding on to hope in hopeless situations has never been more relevant to many than today. I see it as an invitation to be proactive in transfiguring our world.... Our resurrected Lord Jesus Christ was a loser in the eye of the empire, but victorious in our eyes, when we remain, like his disciples, faithful to his message of transformative love for all."

The transformative power of true Christian faith has always been its amazing humility and goodwill, on the model of its Lord Jesus Christ, to forgive, to pray for and love those who persecute it. This is the power of resurrection of light and life which overcomes the powers of darkness and evil.

The moment has come for believing Christians all over the world and people of good will everywhere to rise to save life through their own suffering, and secure justice, peace and joy for all God's creation:

Christ is Risen! he is Risen indeed.

The Fast and the Feast